哲学の庭

The Garden of Philosophy

中村隆重
Takashige Nakamura

東京図書出版

賢者のことばに"人はみな生かされて生きてゆく"とある。
『ダイヤモンド婚を狙え!!』と生涯の友、久幸氏から激励され日々その言葉に励みを得て
暮らしに張りがわいている。

年金暮らしの我が身をもてあます程の時間の余裕と、日々の心のやすらぎが暮らしの中に
ある。

心のゆく先が我が家の庭に行く。表庭には毎年毎年手を加え続け乍らも、裏庭には今ひと
つ納得いかぬ所にやっと手を加えた。加えた飛び石に何回となく足を運ぶたびに、挫折し
た過去の思い出が甦る。

この敷地に従来からあった菩薩像。たどれば八島太郎の生誕地とくる。40年昔、憧れの
この地に３度目の自宅を施工した時、持ち込んだ大石。理事長を息子に譲った３年前移設
した灯篭。
それぞれが飛び石と結び合い過去の出来事が甦ってきた。
つつがなく晩年を迎えられたのは、愛、支え、友情があったればこそと気付くことにな
る。

小生にとって思考を深める場を提供してくれた哲学の庭ともいえる。

中村隆重

PREFACE

A wise man said, "All the people are kept alive." Mr. Hisayuki, my lifelong friend, said, "May you two celebrate your diamond wedding," which cheers me up and brings new vitality to my life.

I'm living on a pension and have enough time, so that I feel greater peace of mind in daily life.

My focus is always turned towards the garden. I have kept the front yard beautiful each year and finally did something to the backyard whereat I have been displeased. Every time I stepped on the stepping stones, that brought back memories of suffering from setbacks.

Those are as follows: the statue of Bodhisattva which had been in this property, the birthplace of Taro Yashima; the big stone which was hauled into this place of longing around forty years ago when I built the third dwelling house; the stone lantern which was moved three years ago when I relinquished my title as chairperson of Shirahatokai to my son. These things evoke my memories of past events in combination with the stepping stones. Now that I'm living happily in my later years, I know for sure that it was all thanks to love, support and friendship.

The space in which I have gained more insight can be called the garden of philosophy.

Takashige

時が来れば 花は必ず咲く

大学受験の失敗
就職試験の失敗
県知的障害者福祉協会会長選2度も落選
旧根占町町長選の落選

幾度の挫折にめげず
耐えて八十路に最高の誉を得る

When the Time Comes, Flowers Inevitably Bloom

Failure in university entrance exams

Failure in employment examination

Losing twice in the election for the chairperson of prefectural association in intellectual disability

Defeat in mayoral contest of former Nejime Town

Despite a number of failures,

The highest honor was earned at the age of eighty after enduring countless hardships

風雪に耐えることで　八十路までの人生が甦る

度重なる落選は強烈なショックであった。
孤独に耐える試練でもあった。
人を恨むことなしに「ナニクソ」……
「意地」と「忍耐」のド根性が培われた。
無欲な努力は自らの成長に繋がったようだ。

Patience and Endurance Make Eighty Years of My Life Burst into Bloom

Repeated electoral defeats gave me a terrific shock.

Those were also trials in which I should endure loneliness.

Without holding a grudge against others, I won't give in . . .

I have acquired plenty of guts and endurance.

Selfless spirit seems to lead to my growth.

２人の刑事課長夫妻からの感激の慰労会

町長選に落選の翌朝、私の運動員の中から、選挙違反者が逮捕され29日間の留置生活を送った。その間の私共夫婦の苦しみは想像を絶するものであったが、それを人に話す勇気はまだなく、また別の機会にすることとして、ここでは滅多にない事を紹介する。

運動員を取り調べた刑事１課長、刑事２課長夫妻から鹿児島市内にある課長宅で接待を受け、花輪まで頂戴した。そこで課長２人が私にした話。「選挙違反の運動員は、ブタ箱生活２日目には応援した候補者への愚痴をぶち明け、自分の過ちから逃れようとする人がほとんどであるにもかかわらず、貴方の運動員は自分の非を認め29日間ずっと候補者に申し訳ないの一点張りで通し切った。このようなケースは刑事生活で初めてであり、私共は人間を信ずることができて感激した。感謝したい」とのことだった。

またその１年後、私自身が違反者を出したにもかかわらず、所轄の警察署長からも最大の称賛の言葉をいただいたことが忘れられない。

The Impressed Celebration Party Held
by Two Detective Section Chiefs and Their Wives

On the following morning I lost in an election for a mayoral contest, two electioneers of my campaign staff were arrested and detained for 29 days. The emotional pain my wife and I felt all that while was imaginable, I don't have the courage to tell that and thus save it for another time. So, I'm going to talk about a rare occurrence.

One day I was hosted as a guest at some chief's house in Kagoshima City by the chiefs of detective section one and two, who investigated the two electioneers, and their wives. Moreover, they gave me a bouquet of flowers. The following is what they said. Most electioneers who committed election violations would put complaints about the candidate they worked for on the next day after they were arrested. They would also try to escape the charge of their guilt. However, my electioneers admitted their guilt, and regretted that they have done me wrong all through the period of detention.

The chiefs said that they experienced such an incident for the very first time in their career as detectives, that they were deeply moved because they could trust humans, and that they wanted to express their appreciation.

I cannot forget that a year after that I was given the highest praise by the chief of the local police, although one of my electioneers committed an election violation.

千代に八千代に　苔の生すまで

４人の子どもが皆東京、大阪そして海外での生活や旅行を経験している。
便利さや賑やかさを追求する時代に過疎化の激しい我が町に帰り住むことは親として「子は宝」と思える。
この流れが孫の代まで１人でも繋がれば神の思し召しとも思える。

Forever and Ever, until Moss Grows Nice and Green

My four children have lived in Tokyo, in Osaka and abroad, and have experienced international travel. In an era when convenience and gaiety are pursued, if children come back their hometown which suffers from depopulation, it seems to every parent that "children are treasure."

If this trend continues, if only a little, to the next generation, it seems to be a message from God.

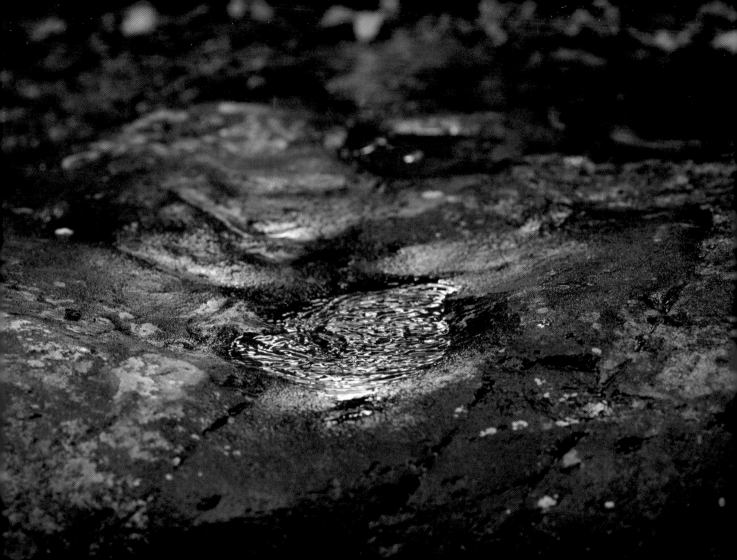

波らん万丈

かぎりない生命力
花の木農場にある彫刻家・速水史朗作「生成」と
感動するものが共通する
　　　　　　　　　　　　　　― 義父からの贈物 ―

Full of Ups and Downs

Unbounded life force
"Generation": sculptor Shiro Hayami fecit, exhibited in Hananoki Farm, Kagoshima
Both move people.

— Gift from my father-in-law —

思わぬ手紙に感謝いっぱい

終戦後の物不足の時代、入学式も経験しなかったアルバムに「もうすぐ小学3年生」と謳った集合写真がある。その時の担任の先生から突然手紙が届いた。

「小生、小学2年生では考えがつかない、76年も昔の恩師である」

社会人となってから一度お会いしただけの疎遠な間柄でありながら、小学2年生の小僧時代のエピソードが手に取るように伝わってきた。

地域再生大賞の受賞を我が事のように喜ぶ姿が伝わる。差出元は佐賀県の老人施設からであり、押し車で生活する状況下での祝福だが、衰えを知らぬ達筆な文面であった。受賞も最高の喜びであったが、その副産物は計り知れない。

四十数年、誹謗中傷はされても、評価されぬ日々を過ごした時代を思うと感激はひとしおであり、晩年に大きな安らぎと達成感をもたらしている。

我が庭を散策しながら心に染みる。終活もまた楽しけりである。

Tremendously Grateful for an Unexpected Letter

There is a group photo titled "Going to Be Third Graders Soon" in the graduation album of my elementary school. At that time the entrance ceremony wasn't held, as we were running short of daily necessities and very poor after the war. My homeroom teacher at the time sent me a letter unexpectedly.

It said, "I was your teacher 76 years ago, though the distant future should have been beyond any stretch of the imagination for the second grader at that time." I have met the former teacher only once since I became an adult, and I lost contact with him. However, the letter included detailed description of the things that happened around me in those days, which reminded me of the days clearly.

I can almost see that he was so happy for my receiving an award of regional revitalization as though he were the one who achieved the award. The sender's address was that of an assisted living facility in Saga prefecture, and he was using a wheelchair. However, the letter was well-written and filled with unflagging energy. Receiving the award brought me a supreme delight, but this side benefit was of inestimable value.

It is notably impressive to have the highest honor and receive a congratulatory letter, because even though I became a target of abuse, I had been given no recognition for forty years. In latter days of my life, I have been given greater peace of mind and a feeling of accomplishment.

When I stroll around the garden, I feel at ease. Making plans and decisions for the end of my life is fun with this garden.

斎藤栄吉氏（富山銀行頭取）との出会い

氏が日本銀行鹿児島支店長時代、私の家に泊まっていただいたことがある。乾杯の挨拶だけで終わりと思われたが、すっかり意気投合した。夜中0時、東京住まいである奥様への定期連絡の電話で私を紹介していただき、明け方4時過ぎまで飲み明かした。

それから盆正月の付け届けをする程につきあいが深まり逝去されるまでの間ずっと続いた。

氏の「庶民性」が今も懐かしく思いだされる。

The Encounter with Eikichi Saito, President of Toyama Bank

I have once offered Mr. Saito accommodation, when he was a manager of Bank of Japan Kagoshima Branch. At a party I had thought that just making a toast was enough, but we hit it off. At twelve midnight, he introduced me to his wife living in Tokyo over the phone as his regular contact. Then we drank the night away until dawn.

Since then, we had sent each other a present gift at the time of Bon festival and the New Year. This gift-giving lasted until his death.

I still recall his "common touch" with fondness.

努力する価値

私は小学生時代、運動会の徒競走は卒業するまでビリから２番目であった。それが悔しくて、運動会が近づくと毎朝練習を繰り返した。その甲斐あって、中学から高校までは１番にはなれなくても、３番をとることができた。
諦めずに努力することの「価値」を思い知ることにもなった。

Significance of Effort

When I was in elementary school, I used to be the second to last in a track meet on sports days. As I felt frustrated, I had a lot of practice every morning as the date of the sports day drew nearer. It was worth it. I was able to be the third in junior high school and senior high school, though I didn't come first.
I appreciate knowing that there is significant value in not giving up and keeping hustling.

花の木農場への目

今から30年も昔のこと、大手航空会社の重役を経験された方から、花の木農場を絶賛されたことがある。私はあまりにも思いがけない見方であったゆえ、自分の負の部分をさらけ出した。すると「組長は誰にでもなれる。しかし、今の花の木農場の開発（姿）は貴方にしかできない」と返ってきた。

その意味するところを、それ以来ずっと考え続けている。

Attention to Hananoki Farm

Three decades ago, Hananoki Farm was acclaimed by a person who had been in an executive position of a leading airline company. As I thought it was totally unexpected reaction, I showed the darker aspects of humanity. Then, he said, "Anyone can be a chief. However, you are the only one who can advance the development of current Hananoki Farm." Since then, I have been thinking about the meaning.

今や我が屋敷

幼少の頃、車がやっと通れるくらいの小路に、他を圧倒する石垣の門があった。
小松帯刀の流れをくむ「おおすみの寒村小根占村野間城」の一角にある、重成知事時代の県議長宅であった。かつてはその路を行き来する度に、仰ぎ見たものである。
さらにその先は八島太郎の生誕地とくる。地域に轟く著名人達の名に恥じない人間となるべく、肝に銘じて求めた土地であった。

Currently My Mansion

When I was a child, there was a magnificent stone wall gate in an alley no wider than a driveway.

It was a home of a prefectural assembly chairman, which was located in a portion of Noma Castle in Konejime Village, Oosumi, Kagoshima, at the time when Mr. Shigenari served as a governor. (Nejime, where Noma Castle was situated, is the place which was governed by the ancestor of Tatewaki Komatsu, a political figure in the last days of the Tokugawa Shogunate.) I used to gaze up at the gate whenever I passed through the alley.

Furthermore, the area in the near distance is the birthplace of Taro Yashima. I have found my current home, fully aware that I must develop a fine personality, so that I live up to their reputation.

思い遣り

私が50歳を過ぎ、年をとった父親に何かと進言した時代、父は受け容れることはなく無言で、自分の行動を変えようとはしなかった。過去の父への進言が今や我が身。子どもからの一言一言が我が身にこたえる。余生を送る境遇となって、相手の気持ちを思う「優しさ」と「厳しさ」が欠如していたことを反省し、遅きに至りながらも、父の気持ちを思い遣る。

悔悟の念に駆られる昨今である。

Thoughtfulness

When I came to make suggestions to my aged father after turning fifty, he wouldn't take my advice without saying anything, and wouldn't change what he was doing. The same suggestions I once made to my father are now directed towards me. Every word my children say pierces me to the bone. It was not until I came to spend the rest of my life that I realized that I was lacking "tenderness" within "strictness" with which I should be thoughtful to others. Although long overdue, now I reflect upon my mistakes and am thinking about my father's feelings. I'm feeling remorse these days.

基希（長女麻子の長男）防大入校記念樹

自ら防大を希望し、自らの立ち位置をわきまえ
頑張る姿を、ジジは快く見守る。

師の君の
いさ諭し深く
胸に抱き
清く正しく
進み行かん
　　麗子

The Commemorative Tree to Celebrate Grandchild's Admission to National Defense Academy

I'm agreeably watching over you who decided for yourself which university you wanted to go to, and would give it your all, remembering your place.

My venerable former teacher's
Meaningful words
Keeping them in mind
With honesty and with integrity
I will step forward

Takiko

羅針盤のおかげ

人から冷たく見られていた農業との取り組みを解決すべく、二十数年前から社会福祉法人と農業法人の両会計の決算報告書までの作業を依頼している公認会計士がいる。氏は信頼にたる会計士で、京都見物を共にする間柄の私の息子に対しても、守秘義務を貫き通した堅物である。それは農業法人について疑問視していた息子が、私が30年もの間、自分の所得から農業法人へつぎ込んでいた実態をつい最近知った程である。

氏の的確な指導は税務署の取り調べで150万円の追徴の通告を受けながらも税務署とのキャッチボールを繰り返しその結果2年間、150万円ずつの返金を受け取ることとなった。

Thanks to the Compass

In order to implement numerous efforts to improve the productivity of agriculture which was disregarded, I have retained a certified public accountant for making the financial results of the social welfare corporation and the agricultural corporation for about twenty years. He is very reliable and I admire his professional attitude towards his work. When he accompanied my son to Kyoto, he completely protected the confidentiality of personal information about me. My son, who had been watching the management of the agricultural corporation suspiciously, lately knew the fact that I had been putting some of my income into the corporation for thirty years.

When the tax office imposed ¥1,500,000 on me for back taxes, he accurately made a thorough survey and conducted tough negotiations with the tax office repeatedly. Consequently, I obtained ¥1,500,000 as a refund for two years.

夢は「天下を取る」

度重なる挫折にも人を恨むことなく、ただ耐えた。

私は他との競争ではなく、「天下を取る」という夢みたいなことを考えて育ってきた。『兎と亀』の亀が兎を競争相手とせず山の頂上を目指し努力したが如く、忍耐強く、そして油断なくコツコツ励むことに置きかえた。

その成果が、比べ物にならない程の大会社のチームを破った、日本産業人バレーボール大会での全国優勝。そして誰でも入ることはできない内閣総理官邸での「ディスカバー農山漁村の宝」受賞。全国地方新聞46社と共同通信社の推薦を受けた50団体の中の最高賞「地域再生大賞」受賞等は晩年に大きな達成感をもたらした。

My Dream: "Getting Ruling Power"

I haven't been discouraged by a succession of setbacks and have endured hardships without holding a grudge against others.

For me the goal of living was not to compete with others, but to get "ruling power" which was rather nebulous. As in the fable of the race between the rabbit and the tortoise, with no thought of competitors I have tried plugging away with patience and with my eyes wide open in order to go for the top.

Thanks to the collective effort, our team came first in a national tournament of company volleyball league, including much larger company teams than ours. We also attended the award ceremony held in Prime Minister's Official Residence, which not everyone can enter. Moreover, we won a grand prize of local development among fifty groups, which were nominated by 46 local newspaper companies and Kyodo News. This brought me a great sense of achievement in my final years.

厄払いの言葉

小学4年生から6年生まで担任だった先生が、私の42歳の厄払いの席での挨拶で、50人を超える客人を前に「隆重の厄は私が引き受ける」とおっしゃった。それから5年が経った昭和61年、私が47歳の時に過疎化の激しい我が町（根占）から鹿児島市進出を図った。希望に燃え、血気盛んな年頃である。それは「職住分離の時代」を見据えてのことである。

その拠点となる翔ビル落成祝いの夜、小生の成功を我が事のように悦んでいただいたその帰路、市電との「衝突事故死」という思いもよらぬ形で現実となった……。

今でも先生との別れが脳裏に焼きついている。

Words for Spiritual Protection

My homeroom teacher in the fourth to sixth grades said, "If bad luck should strike Takashige, I would sacrifice myself for him" in front of more than fifty persons who were present at the gathering for good luck when I was forty-two. Five years later, in 1986, when I was forty-seven, I changed my place of work from my hometown Nejime, which had become sparsely populated, to Kagoshima City. Then I was full of energy and ambition.

In the evening of the inauguration of the new building, he was delighted with my success as if it happened to him. On his way home, he passed away in a collision accident. His words became a reality all of sudden.

The moment of his death burned into my mind, and I still clearly remember that to this day.

黒子に徹した友人

「なにくそ」と、頑固な一徹さで次第に友を失っていった。

一方、陰で私を的確にとらえ、見守っていた人がいたことにも気づくことになる。友人ぶる振る舞いもなく、何時の間にか自然と交流が深まった。その流れによって徐々に気持ちが落ち着くことにも気づいた。

誰からも励まされることのない日々に、自分のとるべき行動の「良し悪し」を判断する時、その人の一言一言が航海する船を導く灯台のごとく、私に光を与えてくれた。

私にとって数少ない理解者であって、事を行う上で大きな勇気を与えてもらった。おかげで彷徨うことなく今日を迎えられた。

Some of My Friends behind the Scene

Because of my stubbornness, the number of friends I have has been decreasing gradually. On the other hand, I came to realize that there had been someone who understood what's inside of me and had been watching me behind the scenes. Since such persons would not pretend to be a friend, we have naturally deepened our bonds. I also noticed that my heart came to feel at ease gradually with them.

On the days, when nobody encouraged me and I had to judge which action I should take, every word from such friends shone a light on me as if lighthouses help ships see where dangerous waters are.

They are only a few people who understand me, and give me a lot of courage when I have to do something. Without their help, I couldn't have come this far without hesitation.

尊い「支え」

東京から数回花の木農場を訪れ、2、3日宿泊して入所者と交流を楽しむ友人がいる。彼は第一観音、第二観音、第三観音と名付け、女性職員の働きぶりに高い称賛を送ってくれる。愛に満ちた職員への評価として有難い。

50年間、無事荒海を乗り越えて、目的地にたどり着いた。

「船長を支える船員がいればこそできる」が如く彼女らは天下取りの野望を達成する「支え」となった女神とも言える。

ただ感謝の日々である。

なお有難くも、我が女房を慈母観音とも褒め称えてくれた。

Precious "Support"

One of my friends in Tokyo sometimes visits Hananoki Farm, and stays for a few days and enjoys mixing with other guests. He calls female staff members first Kannon (meaning Goddess of Mercy), second Kannon, third Kannon and so on, and admires their performance. His heartfelt praise is very valuable.

For fifty years we have overcome the raging waves and have reached our destination. Without the support of the crew the captain cannot control his ship. They seem to be goddesses who support the ambition of my getting ruling power. I'd like to express my thanks and gratitude every day.

In addition, I'm grateful that he also called my wife Jibokannon, i.e., Goddess of Mercy.

父母からの愛

母は私の蛮行や挫折を温かく見守ってくれた。そのことは他に比べられるものはなく、私の将来への可能性をも信じ切ってくれたこともまた然りである。それは愛そのものでしかない。

父にしても、晩年まで何かと立ち向かった事が多々あったが父の死後に振り返って考えると、今日の私の礎は父の協力のもとに築かれている。度重なる多額の借入金の保証人であり、また立ち向かう相手との戦いの時には、常に私の味方であった。

２人からの愛が、最大且つ最高のものであったことは、晩年に気づくこととなる。

Love of My Parents

My mother always watched over my rough behavior and setbacks. That was beyond comparison and the same is true of her belief in my future success. That is absolutely her love.

As to my father, although it is true that we had different views on various points, my fundamental human values have been formed on the basis of his cooperation. When I had to borrow much money, he was always my guarantor. When I had to compete against opponents, he was always on my side.

It is in my later years that I realized that love of my parents had been greatest and deepest.

誰も出来ない兄の生き方

兄がこの冬に長期入院をした。妻に先立たれ、不憫に思えてならず、また年金暮らしとは言え、独り身のあわれな姿は見るに忍びなく、我が娘を通して思い切った見舞いを渡した。すると３ヶ月後に退院した時、ヨレヨレの見舞い袋が帰ってきた。入院中、懐に抱いたまま故のシワであった。「これ以上甘えることは出来ない」という佳子（兄の娘）からの進言を受け、兄の意地でもあろうと私は受けとり、兄の自尊心の高さに改めて感服した。

毎日毎日訪ねて声かけを続けたが、兄は誰の悪口も言わず、不平も言わない。「自立の姿」に、同情を通り越し「達観した生き方」として、我も見習う「見本」と敬服する日々である。

My Brother's Way of Living Not Everyone Can Choose

My brother was hospitalized over a long period this winter. He was predeceased by his wife. I cannot help feeling sorry for him. As it was heartbreaking to see a pathetic bachelor, I made my daughter take get-well money to him, though he was living on pensions. Then three months later, the small envelope, which was wrinkled because he had kept it on his chest in bed, was returned. As his daughter said, "We cannot rely on you anymore," I regarded the reaction as his pride, and accepted the envelope. I had so much respect for his pride again.

I visited and talked to him every day, but he never spoke badly of others and never complained. I notice how philosophically he views his life, by watching his independence. I should not sympathize with him. Rather, I should learn from his way of living, and have a great regard for him.

新刊本に寄せて

一度、目指したら変わることがない。まさしく薩摩の「ぼっけもん」。

こう書いてしまったのは、今から15年前、社会福祉法人「白鳩会」を設立されて35年を迎える頃であった。豪快で鋭い語りの間には、周りの方々への多くの感謝や、深く細やかな感性が溢れ出て、広く温かな心が見え隠れする。

「母は、とても愛情深く育ててくれました。小さなころから『どんな子どもでも、皆、神の子なんですよ』と口癖のように言っておりましたね。そして、これがわたしの福祉への思想の原点なのです」

薩摩人らしい磊落ともいえる語り口、そして、高き理想を己の手でしっかりと具現化する力強い生き方、真摯で実直な眼差し。とにかく圧倒されるほどのパワフルな行動力で、自立できる福祉施設を牽引されてきた中村隆重さん。今や日本を代表する福祉事業の先駆者と称され、数々の賞を受賞されながらも決して驕ることなく、鹿児島県大隅半島の最南端の地で、障がいある者と大地をつなぎ、地域を元気にする活動を続ける。この永遠の青年は、福祉の活動を地域づくりまで発展させながらも、未だに地道に活動を続けておられるのだ。

多くの人を惹きつけてやまない中村さんにご友人たちが自叙伝を書くように勧められている現場に居合わせたことがある。きっとその力がこの新刊発行の原動力になったのだろう。薩摩で言う「ぼっけもん」がどのように語られているか、今から私も楽しみである。

地域振興誌「みちくさ」編集長　福永栄子

福永栄子

2000年に東京から南九州に移り住み、日本人の原風景が今なお残る奥日本の風土や魅力を、地域内外の方々にお伝えしてゆきたい、そしてこの魅力を次世代にまで残したいと地域振興誌「みちくさ」を創刊し23年。人と人、地域と地域を「愛」でつなぐ㈱アイロード、エコツアー旅行会社「㈱アイロード・プラス」代表取締役。

花の木農場のあゆみ

昭和48年　社会福祉法人白鳩会設立
昭和53年　農事組合法人根占生産組合設立
昭和60年　毎日新聞主催全国花いっぱいコンクール最優秀賞受賞
昭和63年　全国心身障害者愛のステージで演奏。三笠宮特別賞受賞
平成 9 年　日本産業人バレーボール全国大会優勝
平成20年　根占生産組合農林水産省経営局長賞受賞
平成27年　「ディスカバー農山漁村の宝」優良事例に選出
平成27年　「日本でいちばん大切にしたい会社」審査員特別賞受賞
平成29年　第68回南日本文化賞受賞
令和 3 年　ノウフク・アワード2020グランプリ受賞
令和 3 年　第54回MBC賞受賞
令和 4 年　GAP実践大賞2022受賞
　　　　　　2022年度共同通信社主催　地域再生大賞受賞
令和 5 年　安全安心なまちづくり（再犯の防止等に関する活動）内閣総理大臣表彰

中村　隆重（なかむら　たかしげ）

花の木農場参与
社会福祉法人白鳩会　前理事長

写真：前田利行（まえだ　としゆき）
英訳：濱崎孔一廊（はまさき　こういちろう）

哲学の庭

2023年12月31日　初版第1刷発行

著者
中村隆重

発行者
中田典昭

発行所
東京図書出版

発行発売
株式会社 リフレ出版
〒112-0001　東京都文京区白山5-4-1-2F
電話 (03)6772-7906　FAX 0120-41-8080

印刷
株式会社 ブレイン

© Takashige Nakamura
ISBN978-4-86641-708-0 C0095
Printed in Japan 2023

落丁・乱丁はお取替えいたします。
ご意見、ご感想をお寄せ下さい。